JACK and the GIANT-KILLER AND JACKWITCH

MICHAEL LAWRENCE

TONY ROSS

A PAIR OF
JACKS

ORCHARD BOOKS
338 Euston Road, London NW1 3BH
Orchard Books Australia
Level 17/207 Kent Street, Sydney, NSW 2000
First published in hardback in 2009 by Orchard Books
First published in paperback in 2010
ISBN 978 1 84616 750 8 (hardback)
ISBN 978 1 40830 774 8 (paperback)

A CIP catalogue record for this book is available from the British Library.
1 3 5 7 9 10 8 6 4 2 (hardback)
1 3 5 7 9 10 8 6 4 2 (paperback)
Printed in Great Britain
Orchard Books is a division of Hachette Children's Books,
an Hachette UK company.
www.hachette.co.uk

In days of old when nights were cold and mornings balmy, there lived in the land of Cornwall a youth by the name of Jack, who gained a reputation

as a **slayer** of giants.

But this story isn't

about **that** Jack.

It's about a much later one who would have given an arm, a leg or a kidney for any name but that of the great hero

who killed giants.

Why?

Because this Jack

was a giant.

It was an odd name for giant parents to give their giant son, but Jack's folks had laughed at the old stories. Goblin tales were made up to give young giants nightmares, they always claimed, and named their son Jack to show their disdain.

It wasn't until he reached early gianthood that Jack first heard how his famous namesake had harried and hewn large gentle souls with names like Cormoran, Blunderbore, Thunderdell and Galligantus. And unlike his parents he believed the tales.

And wept.

O, the disgrace, forced to bear the cursed name of such a little villain!

Such was Jack's sensitivity on this issue that, fearing ridicule, he refused to set another foot outside his native land or dally with giants of other regions.

This was fine while his parents were still about – their presence meant there was always someone to shout at him for being such a big sissy – but when they very selfishly popped their gigantic clogs within a week of one another Jack found himself unexpectedly alone in the world.

Father went first, when his whaling boat capsized following a giant belch (a pod of orcas shared him out for lunch), but Mother's end quickly followed when she missed her footing while dusting the battlements one lovely morning in May.*

* The only plus to Mother's demise was that her screaming nosedive saved Jack the trouble of digging a grave for her.

Mother's departure was particularly upsetting for the young giant. He sobbed for days wondering where the next meal was coming from.

But one dismal day, while leafing sentimentally through her old recipe books in the castle kitchen, it dawned on him that if he followed the instructions he too might be able to prepare meals. So he gave it a try, and to his surprise discovered a natural flair for what serious educational establishments

like to call

'food technology'

and his mother

called 'cooking'.

But being a whiz in the kitchen isn't everything, especially when there's no one to cook for but yourself, and loneliness came dark and tall for Jack, especially at night when the castle was

so **gloomy**

and **silent**.

Indeed, there were times when he missed company so badly that he considered following Mother's example and dusting the battlements.

Fortunately,

he dusted the ornaments *instead*, and that's when he found that as well as being a fantastic cook he was really terrific at sprucing things up. Thrilled to have discovered yet another skill, Jack at once set about spring-cleaning the castle from turret to dungeon, and while he was at it undertook several other satisfying tasks as well, such as grouting.

One day, when Jack was least expecting it, something happened that at first seemed quite spectacular to him. He was running the washday sheets through the mangle in the yard when he heard the *thud-thud-thud* of clod-hopping feet. He looked up and saw, galumphing over the hill, a walloping great giantess as wide as three elephants strapped together and as ugly as sixty sins.

For Jack it was **love** at first gasp.

He invited her to tea, congratulating himself on having only the night before baked an ovenful of fairy cakes, each with a dead fairy on top.

The giantess's name was Erthrulda Bogg. When he heard it Jack clasped his fists to his chest with joy. What a melodic moniker! When she asked his name in return he thought of giving a false one, but lying did not come easily to young Jack, and he confessed with downcast eyes. Erthrulda was horrified to learn that he bore the name of their race's greatest scourge, but she was a practical giantess. Jack had a castle and she did not.

In fact, she didn't even have a pot to...

well, you know.

So she **moved in.**

Jack was dizzy with delight when Erthrulda took over the running of the household and his life. Her frightful foghorn voice thrilled him as it **nagged** him from dawn to dusk and dusk to dawn.

So happy was he to no longer be alone, in the company of someone who wore Rotting Horseflesh (a perfume), that he beamed at her every jeer and jibe. 'Call yourself a giant?' Erthrulda would bellow. 'Whoever heard of a giant who likes putting up shelves and making soup? Shame on you, you whose name I can't bear to say! Shame!' Hearing such words from that odious gap-toothed trap, Jack entwined his giant fingers behind

his giant back and giggled with giant glee.

But his happiness was not to last. It ended the morning Giant Depardieu waded over from France on a day-return.

'He's magnificent!' Erthrulda Bogg drooled when Depardieu's crusty plates of meat shook the shore, and clumped off to introduce herself without ado.

'His breath is like fifty dungheaps!' she cooed on her return. 'His lugholes are like two black caverns of Hell!

And what a nose!

I've never seen so much hairy snot in a pair of nostrils!'

At the end of the afternoon the love of Jack's life lumbered down the beach hand in hand with Giant Depardieu, and waded out of his life forever. In other words,

Erthrulda

bogged off.

Most of Jack's time over the weeks following his love's departure was spent moping about the castle or sitting on his mother's giant gravestone ripping the feathers out of parked birds and saying over and over, 'She loathes me, she loathes me not, she loathes me, she loathes me not.'

But then something else happened. Something even **bigger** than the appearance and betrayal of Erthrulda. And this something was to change Jack's life and character **forever**.

He'd been out scouring the countryside for shepherds. Disappointed when he could only find four (according to *Home Cooking for Giants* you needed five for a decent shepherds pie), he dashed the quartet's brains out humanely on a rock, hung them from his belt by their hair, and lumbered home. In the kitchen he stripped and washed the filthy little peasants and put them

through the mincer.

Then he cut up a dozen onions, bawled his eyes out for a minute or two, diced a row of carrots from the vegetable garden, added a barrel of herbs, boiled and mashed the spuds, and popped the dish in the oven.

While waiting for the pie to cook he swept the floors. There were a lot of floors in the castle and it was the first time he'd swept them since Erthrulda left, so it took a while.

He'd almost finished when he heard a knock at the front door. It wasn't much of a knock, yet it sent Jack's hairy eyebrows flying like a brace of startled squirrels.

He never had visitors.

Never.

Who could it be, who, who? But then he had a delirious thought. Erthrulda. She'd come back to give him another piece of her mind! He dropped his broom, smoothed the wrinkles out of his pinny, and yanked the door back.

It wasn't Erthrulda.

It was a human youth clad in doublet and hose.*

Jack whimpered pitifully and wrung his hands. Humans were fine if lightly grilled or poached and served with green salad, but what did you talk to them about?

* That's not a garden hose in case you wonder.

'Sorry to bother you,' said the youth, gazing up at him, 'but I'm looking for a giant and I was wondering if you could help me.'

Jack flinched. 'A giant? Why? What for? Who are you?'

The lad indicated the sword scabbarded at his belt. 'Jim's the name. I'm a giant-killer.'

Hearing this, a mighty dread seized Jack by the scruff of the neck and shook him like an inflated kitten. 'Excuse me,' he said, 'but I think my pie's burning.'

He slammed the door, bolted it, threw three heavy chains across it, and set a chair against it hoping the giant-killer would lose interest and stroll away whistling.

Some minutes passed in this quiet fashion. But then there was another rap of small knuckles on the door.

'Hello in there!
How's the pie?'

'Just saved it,' said Jack in a voice strangely high-pitched for him. 'You, er, kill giants, you say? Unusual profession in this day and age, giant-killing.'

'Not much call for it nowadays,' young Jim replied through the wood. 'Dying breed, giants. But I was brought up on the derring-do of Jack the Giant-Killer and I always longed to have exploits like his. When I heard there was a giant in these parts I saw my chance to cleave his head from his shoulders, and here I am.'

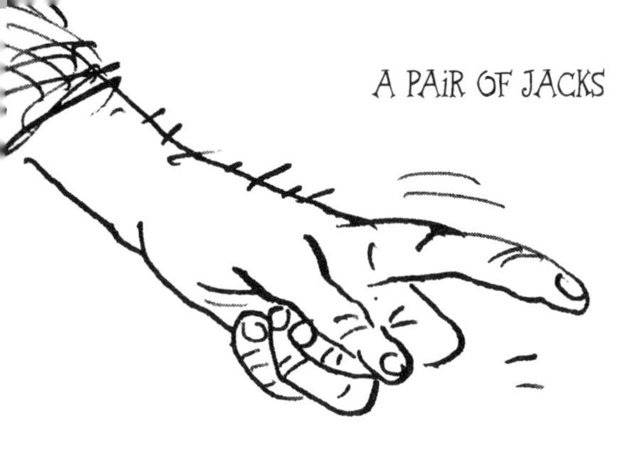

Jack's heart thudded. That name! The name of the cruel murderer of those poor giant innocents of old, which it was his burden and humiliation to share!

'You've been misinformed,' he said as steadily as he was able. 'No giants round here.' But then it came to him how he might throw the boy off his scent. 'No, wait! I've just remembered. There was a giant. Two actually, a male and a female. Went to France. That's where *you* want to look: France.'

'So I've wasted my time,'

said the would-be

giant-killer.

'Seems so,' said Jack.

'Such a journey too, and I haven't eaten since yesterday. Your pie smells good. What sort is it?'

'Shepherds pie. My speciality. The trick is to leave out the apostrophe.'

'Ooh, I love shepherds pie,' said Jim. 'My mum makes the best in our village.'

'Really?' said Jack. 'Well, I hope she has more luck finding shepherds than I do.'

To his surprise this met with a shout of laughter, and: 'That's a good one! Must tell Mum that when I get home. Ha-ha-ha! Hee-hee-hee.'

'What did I say?' Jack said, nonplussed.

'You couldn't spare a hungry stranger a piece of your pie before he goes on his way, could you?' Jim asked when he'd laughed his fill. 'If there's enough, that is.'

Now Jack was as familiar with the old tales as was the youth on the step. The merciless giant-killer of the bad old days had gained entry to giants' homes by all manner of sly devices, and once inside their heads had been off in a jiffy, or their gentle hearts cut out before their great popping eyes. Suppose this boy was trying to trick his way in to deal with him in such a way?

'How do I know this isn't a ruse?' he said to the door.

'What's a ruse?' enquired Jim on the other side of it.

'A cunning wile,' said Jack.

'A wile?' said Jim.

'A mean scheme,' said Jack.

'To do what?' said Jim.

'To get in here and hack my head off,' said Jack.

'Why would I want to do that?' said Jim. 'I've come looking for a giant, not someone who just happens to be rather tall and broad. Come, good sir, let me in and give me a piece of your wonderful pie.'

'You don't think

I'm a **giant** then?'

said Jack.

'You, a giant?' said Jim. 'What an absurd idea. You! A giant! Ha-ha-ha! Hee-hee-hee.'

'Oh, well, in that case,' Jack replied, removing the great chair, releasing the three great chains, drawing the great bolt and opening the great door. 'I'll have to ask you to leave the sword outside, though. Sorry. House rule of my late mother's. No weapons in the castle.'

'No problem!' said Jim,
driving his sword
into the mud by the step.

Jack brought him in and looked out some of the crockery and cutlery his Action-Giant toys had played with when he was no taller than a bungalow. He then lifted Jim onto one of the kitchen stools, but even standing at full stretch the youth could not reach the tabletop, so Jack added a stack of Mother's cookbooks to the seat.

'Better?' he said when Jim had climbed up the books and stood upon *The All-Human Diet* by Slewthem O. Thumpingbutt.

'Much,' said Jim the giant-killer. 'Thank you.'

Jack now removed the perfectly cooked pie from the oven and cut two portions, a tiny one for his little guest and a giant one for himself.

'What do you think of giants anyway?' Jim asked as they tucked in.

'Pretty evil lot, eh?'

'Oh, they're not all bad,' Jack replied carefully. 'They don't kill ants, for instance.'

'Ants?' said Jim, puzzled.

'Humans kill ants,' Jack explained. 'I mean WE humans kill ants. Deliberately. Stamp, stamp, stamp, wipe out whole colonies at a time, just because they're there.

Giants only kill for

their table, usually.

How's the pie?'

Jim munched on. 'Even better than my mum's,' he said appreciatively.

'You don't think one more shepherd would have improved it?' Jack asked.

'There you go again!' his visitor cried with delight. 'One more shepherd! I never knew giants had a sense of humour!'

Jack dropped his fork in shock.

'I'm not a giant, I'm just tall and broad, you said so yourself!'

At this the lad stopped laughing and leapt onto the table. Then, while Jack was still blinking in astonishment, he reached down the back of his shirt and drew forth an exact twin of the sword left quivering in the mud without!

'Not a giant!' said Jim. 'What do you take me for? No one could be as big as you and live in a castle this huge with a table so high if he were not a giant!'

Jack stared in dismay at the sword-point a whisker from his nose. 'So it was a trick.'

'Yes, sorry about that,' Jim said. 'You don't seem such a bad fellow, and you cook so well, but you're a giant and I must slay you, it's the way it works.'

Jack chewed this over with the last of his mouthful. The lad was right.

It was a fact of life.

Boy meets giant,

boy kills giant,

end of story.

He sighed a sigh that rattled the walls.

'How do you want me?' Jack asked.

'Sorry?' said Jim.

'Well, if I have to be slain I think we might as well get it over with.'

'Oh, I see. Well seeing as we're up here, why don't you just place your head on the table? That way I'll be able to get a good swipe at the back of your neck and with any luck your head'll come off with a single blow.'

'Right-oh,' said Jack and he settled his head on the table between the plates and condiment pots.

'You know, I thought it would be harder than this,' Jim said. 'Thought you'd fly into a rage and wield a great club with nails in the end and try and get me first or something.'

'Oh, not me,' Jack said to the tabletop. 'I'm more a DIY type than a fighter. That's why the love of my life stomped out on me. Not giantly enough.'

'Ah well, never mind,' the youth said, and, hoisting his sword, made ready to strike. Before doing so, however, he began to chant, in the deepest, most heroic voice he could muster:

'Fee,
fi,
fo,
fum,
I smell the fluff
of a giant's bum!
Be he—'

'What's that all about?' Jack interrupted.

'It's my giant-killing chant,' Jim told him proudly.

Jack was surprised. 'In the stories I heard it was the giants who chanted, not their killers.'

Jim lowered his sword. 'Yes, same here, and it really ticked me off. Why should giants have all the best chants, I thought. So I wrote one of my own.

'What do you think
of it so far?'

'To tell you the truth, I'm not totally sure about the fluff of a giant's bum bit,' Jack said. 'There's no fluff on my bum. Wasn't last time I looked anyway.'

'This is a chant about giants in general,' said Jim, 'not you specifically.'

'Do most giants have fluff

on their bums then?' Jack enquired.

Jim shrugged. 'No idea. I've never seen a giant's bum. It's just a chant. I had to say something. Listen to the rest of it.'

Jack put his forehead on the table and Jim completed his chant.

'Fee,

fi,

fo,

fum,

I smell the fluff

of a giant's bum!

Be he a fast one or be he stiller

He'll be sorry he met

THIS giant-killer!'

There was a pause when he'd finished, until Jim said: 'Well?'

'Well what?'

'What's the verdict?'

'Oh, sorry, didn't know you wanted my opinion. I thought it was your pre-head-lopping chant and that you were going to lop mine off the moment you'd finished.'

'That was the plan,' said Jim. 'But you're my first actual giant, so I'm quite keen to hear your reaction.'

'Well, I think it's quite…catchy,' Jack said diplomatically.

'You do?'

'Yes. Put a nice tumpy-tump tune to it and you could release it as a free download.'

'You're very kind,' said Jim.

'Don't mention it,' said Jack.

Jim raised his sword again. 'All set?' he asked.

'Mm.'

Gritting his teeth and clenching his buttocks for the mighty swipe that would send Jack's great head rolling off the table and onto the floor, Jim was about to do the dreadful deed when he thought of something and lowered his sword once more.

'I almost forgot,' he said.

'What?'

'Giant-killers need the names of their victims so they can boast about who they've killed to everyone they meet for years to come. It's no good just saying "I killed this ferocious giant". You have to give the name of the giant or no one believes you. Giants have fantastic names. Names to curdle the blood and give impressionable kids the runs. I bet yours is pretty blood-curdling, isn't it?'

'Not really,'
Jack admitted quietly.

Jim's eyes filled with bright visions of glory.

'Think of it! You'll be almost as famous as me! For centuries to come people will be talking about how I sliced your head off and dragged it home to be kicked by the villagers, worried by the dogs, and sucked clean by the flies.'

'That's good to know,' said Jack.

'So what is it?'

'What's what?'

'Your name.'

Jack shifted about uncomfortably. Did he really have to give his name – that name – to his human executioner?

'If it's all the same to you, I'd rather keep it to myself,' he said.

'Oh, don't be shy,' said Jim. 'We've come this far. All you have to do is say your name and we're done. Well, **YOU** are.'

Jack lifted his head. 'The fact is, you'd be better off making up a name than telling people mine.'

'Oh, I couldn't do that, it would be cheating. Look, tell you what. The moment you spit out your name I'll bring my sword down – **SWISH!**

'Your head'll be off so fast

that you won't have time

to think about *it*.'

'That's very considerate of you,' said Jack. 'But you'll be disappointed if I tell you, and possibly even a tad miffed.'

'I'll risk it,' said Jim.

'Very well. But make sure you end this with one clean swipe.'

'You have a pretty thick neck,' Jim said, 'but I'll do my best.'

Jack got back into position, forehead on table top, and braced himself for a cockroach-eye view of the floorboards without even getting off his chair. Jim raised his sword.

'OK. In your
own time.
Tell me
your name.'

'My name,' Jack said slowly, 'my name is...'

(He really was very embarrassed about this.)

'Yes?' said Jim.

'Are you sure you want to hear it?'

'Yes. Absolutely.'

'Well then, it's...'

'Yes?'

'Jack.'

'What?'

'My name. It's Jack.'

'Jack? You're pulling my leg.'

'No. Honestly.'

'But that's the name of the greatest giant-killer of all time!' cried Jim.

'I know. Awfully sorry.'

'A giant simply cannot bear his name!' Jim said despairingly.

Jack raised his head. 'I did warn you. I said you wouldn't be pleased.'

'How can I kill someone who bears the name of my hero, even if he is a giant?' Jim wailed. 'It's impossible! I just can't do it!'

With this the distraught youth hurled the sword clear of the table. It fell on the cold stone floor, where it lay rattle-rattle-rattling away to nothing.

Jack sat up. 'Have some more pie,' he offered by way of consolation. 'That bit there looks good. More shepherd than the rest.'

A light appeared in the boy's eye. The corners of his mouth flipped up. He began to laugh.

'There you go again! More shepherd than the rest! You should be on the stage, you know that?'

Jack frowned. 'I don't see what's so funny.'

'And now that I've got over the shock,' Jim went on, 'it's quite a hoot that you, a giant, should be called after someone who made his name by killing giants!

Jack the Giant.

Oh boy.

Oh boy,

oh boy,

oh boy!'

Jack's thumbs twitched involuntarily. His eyebrows reached for the bridge of his nose and wrestled one another over the side. He could take a little laughter at his expense, but there was a limit. Making fun of him for having that name was out of order. Way out!

The eyes of the youth on the table were filled with joyful tears that jumped over his lashes and hiccupped down his cheeks.

'Jack the Giant!' he chortled. 'Jack the Giant!' (He was really milking this.)

'You'll be the death of me, Giant.
The death of me!
Ha-ha-ha!
Hee-hee-he—

He broke off in mid 'hee' because Jack had reached for him, bitten his head off, and spat it at a passing rat.

'Fee, fi, fo, fum,' said Jack when this was done.

I'm very pleased to report that from that day forth, Jack was a changed giant. No longer did he mope about the castle missing company, and he stopped being ashamed of his name – in fact was rather proud of it now. So proud indeed that he hammered a big sign over the castle entrance to tell the world who he was, and what his line of work might be should the need to earn a living ever arise.

Jack the
Giant-Killer
Killer

No more giant-killers ever came knocking on Jack's door, but word got out about Jim's fateful visit, and it soon became common knowledge that the castle was home to a creature as ferocious and bloodthirsty as any of the fabled giants of yore. Jack was now feared the length and breadth of the land without even taking his pinny off, and he was rather proud of that. It made him feel...

well, like a **proper giant** at last!

JACKWITCH

Grimm the woodcutter never smiled. Nor did his son Jack. They didn't talk much either, and as for singing and dancing it was as if they'd never heard of such things.

'Grimm by name,
grim by nature,'
people would say of them.

Only at Hallowe'en did things get a bit livelier in the Grimm household, for then Jack's father would hang the windows with mistletoe and garlic and nail a horseshoe over the door to keep the witches out. And when this was done he would say to Jack: 'You stay put, boy. I'm going out for an hour to see if I can't catch me a witch.'

If Grimm ever did catch
a witch he never brought her
home, or even spoke of the catching,
which greatly disappointed young Jack, who
longed to see one in the flesh and
thrill to the tale of how
she'd been snared.

It wasn't until the evening of his thirteenth birthday (which happened to fall on Hallowe'en night) that he resolved to see a witch with his own eyes, come what may, and when his father set off through the woods he followed.

It was dark amid the trees, but silver imps of moonlight danced among the tangled branches, providing just enough light for Jack to see his father striding ahead, his great axe slung over his shoulder. No sound was there, no sound at all, until an owl hooted in some distant pocket of the night, whereupon, as if at a signal, a wind jumped up and the trees began a-creaking and a-whispering, and Jack, head bent against the gale, lost sight of his father.

The windy night closed in, all creaky, all whispery, but on Jack went, step by ginger step, till he came to a certain oak, where he found, buried deep in the ancient trunk, the woodsman's axe.

'What happened to Father?' he cried in alarm. 'Have the witches got him?'

As if in answer he heard thin, sharp, scratchety voices up ahead, and as he heard them the high wind dropped to its knees and expired. In the sudden stillness, Jack moved forward with stealth to stand behind an evergreen bush at a clearing's edge.

In the clearing, meekly illuminated by a cloud-draped moon, were gathered the oddest group of individuals imaginable.

All dressed in snub-nosed, dull-buckled shoes they were, and black crumpled hats with chewed rims, and matching robes that failed to flow. Most had alarmingly long noses and fingers like knotted pipe cleaners, and each one held a broomstick cut from local ash, with twigs of birch bound up with willow twine.

'Witches!' Jack whispered in both dread and triumph.*

* Some of the gathered were, in fact, warlocks, though they were just as ugly and also carried broomsticks.

From his hiding place Jack watched the witches take turns to dip a finger into a large pot, dab their foreheads, mount their broomsticks (brush part foremost, as real witches do), and with a joyful shout of

'Up and up, out and about!'

hurtle towards the raggedy clouds that veiled the face of the witch in the moon.

Soon there was but one left upon the ground, and Jack craned for a better look as the final witch reached for the dabbing pot. As he craned, however, something brittle snapped beneath his foot (as something often does in surreptitious moments) and the witch whirled and glared into the darkness.

'Come out, come out,
whatever you are.
If you be witch then fly with me,
but if you be other...aaah!'

Keen to seem bolder than he felt, Jack had stepped from his leafy hiding place. The witch's bony shoulders shuddered at the sight of the birthday boy.

'Eeergh!' said she.
'A revolting human child.'

Then she leant forward. 'Well, brat, prepare to become a...let me see, what shall it be? Ah. Yes. A hedgehog, I think.'

'A hedgehog?' said Jack. 'Oh, I don't think I'd like that. I mean hedgehogs are hedgehogs and boys are boys, and I quite like being a boy.'

'Your likes and dislikes have nothing to do with it,' rasped the hag, who then began to enunciate the spell that makes prickly hedgehogs of smooth-fleshed boys.

She was halfway through her malevolent chant when Jack felt something warm and soft winding itself about his legs. The witch lowered her hoary old spell finger.

'But you have a familiar!' she cried with incredulity. 'A human with a familiar? It's **unheard** of!'

Jack bent down and tickled the night-black creature behind the ear. 'Oh, this is just an old cat I see prowling the woods sometimes.'

'Tsss!' hissed the witch. 'That's no ordinary cat. A witch can tell these things. You are touched by the Magic, boy, or it wouldn't let you near its ears. Well then, clearly I must leave you be!'

With that she dabbed her forehead, hauled a bony ankle over the shaft of her besom*, and up she flew to join her associates weaving in and out of the raggedy clouds that veiled the face of the witch in the moon.

Jack stepped further into the clearing and read the label on the pot the witches had left behind.

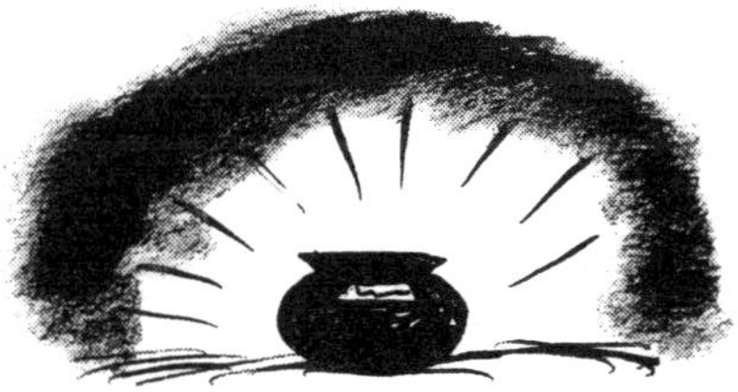

* Her broom.

'Would you like to fly, lad?' enquired a smooth voice at his feet.

Jack looked down. The cat gazed up at him, green eyes a'glow as if lit from within.

'Was that you, cat? Can you speak?'

'I can,' said the cat, preening itself.

'Well I never!'

'Why not dab some of that ointment on yourself?' the cat suggested.

'Oh, I couldn't do that,' said Jack, though tempted.

'Go on. Be a devil.'

'Well. . .all right. Just a little.'

And he dipped a finger in the pot of Flying Ointment and dabbed his brow – and at once he felt as light as eiderdown.

'Now all you need is something to fly on,' the cat said.

'I haven't got a broomstick,' said Jack.

'Oh you don't need a broomstick with me here!'

So saying, the cat began to grow, and on it grew, and on, till it was half Jack's height. Struck dumb, Jack simply stared.

'Hop onto my back,' said the cat.

Jack hopped on.

'Now grip the fur around my neck,' said the cat.

Jack gripped the furry neck and the cat leapt up, and very soon they were watching the stars punch their way through the fabric of the night as, like the broomsticked ones before them, they wove in and out of the raggedy clouds that veiled the face of the witch in the moon.

'Do you know what hour this is?' the cat said as they flew.

'All I know is that it's late and I shouldn't be out,' Jack answered.

'It is the Hour of Gathering, when the Charmed Ones assemble before the Grand Master and tell of the mischief they've created this past twelve-month.'

'Who's the Grand Master?' Jack asked.

To this the cat made no reply, and they flew on in silence.

Time passed, but not much of it, before Jack saw, far below, a great circle of flickering light – a bonfire, round which dark figures stood with their familiars: cats and rats, frogs and dogs, weasels with measles, and many a black bird with fidgety wings. And no creature there, he noticed, not one – animal, rodent, bird or witch or warlock – cast the slightest hint of a shadow.

As the cat began its descent Jack became nervous. 'Cat, are you sure we ought to go down there? I mean there's no telling what they'll do if they see me.'

'It will be entertaining to find out,' was the amused reply.

When the cat's four paws struck earth, Jack climbed off its back. As all eyes turned his way, widening with disbelief, the cat withdrew from the circle of flickering light.

A scrawny witch sidled up and touched Jack's cheek, wincing at its smoothness. 'What's this?' she said.

'How came you here, **human**?'

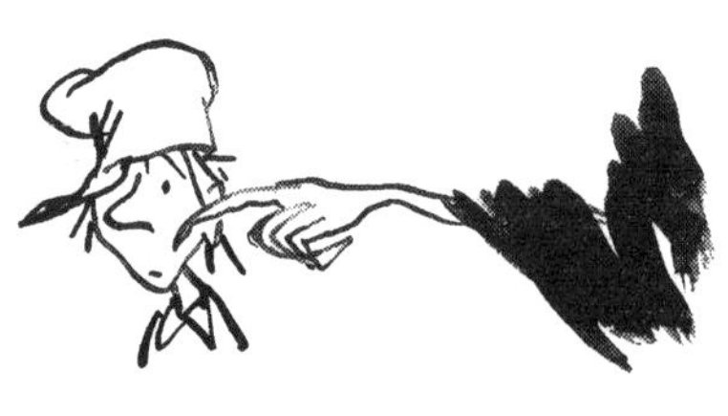

'I...I flew, madam,' said Jack, doing his best not to tremble.

'Flew?' The witch curled a lip of skinny disdain.

'Humans don't *fly*.

Humans can't *fly*.

Humans are useless, pointless creatures!' she said.

Others now
clustered round
to pinch his cheeks
and tug his ears and pluck
his clothes.

'Pop it in the pot,' said one.
'Boy stew, pasty but tasty.'

'Bubble it up with
knotweed, patchouli,
yarrow and rue,' said
another.

'Serve it soft and soggy with
warty witch bread,' said a third.

Then they were grabbing him and dragging him to the enormous cauldron of water that witches warm up on such occasions in case a rare delicacy such as 'boy' happens by. Beyond the ring of firelight the cat watched as Jack was tossed into the warming water; continued to watch as he spluttered up and salt and herbs were sprinkled on his head; listened as the eager witches and warlocks began to chant:

'Boil it good and salt it well,
Heat it through and carve it clean,
Come the dawn the bones we'll sell,
Of Boy Feast this Hallowe'en!'

But as the chant concluded a great black shape rose up and blocked out the cloud-draped moon and the stars and constellations beyond.

'LEAVE THE CHILD!'

It was the cat grown huge, towering over all and everything, claws spread like rows of honed scimitars, tail lashing like an angry ogre's whip, eyes as bright as beacons of green fire.

The gathering fell to its collective knees. 'Grand Master!' cried every voice in awe.

'Grand Massshter?' spluttered Jack in the cauldron. 'The cat?'

'The boy is one of us!' roared the monstrous feline.

'But sir,' a small warlock at the back ventured, 'he's...human.'

'Look again!' said Grand Master Cat.

They looked again.

'Well, what do you know,' one witch said.

'And to think we nearly ate him,' said another.

'Oooo,' said Jack, as well he might, for his nose was extending awkwardly and his hair turning coarse as neglected thatch, his pure features lumpen and spotty.

'Hoick him out at once!' Grand Master Cat commanded.

They hauled Jack out of the cauldron, rather more gently than they'd tumbled him in, and...his shadow did not come with him!

'He **is** one of us,' murmured the gathered.

'He's more than one of you,' the big cat said. 'The night will come when he'll be more powerful than any here.'

'Please explain, Grand Master,' they beseeched as they dried Jack off with hankies doused in witch-hazel.

To which the cat would say nothing but 'Meeeooow!' before giving the order for the festivities to begin. Then bedraggled hats were thrown in the air, buttocky warts were scratched till they bled, a warlock produced a catgut fiddle and ghastly dirges were screeched while Charmed Ones danced atrociously.

During all this Jack stood with the cat, which had made itself small again, if not as small as cats usually are, and when the dancing was over, all present recited their year's Mischief; and when the Witching Hour was up and a new chant was uttered by the throng – 'Returnum backum, homeward bounden' – the revellers dispersed in ones and twos, in gaggles and covens, and up, up, up they flew, into the fragile frosty sky, till Jack and the cat stood alone by the embers of the dying fire.

'Come, lad,' the cat said, growing large again. 'It's time you were a'bed. Hop on!'

There were no witches in the clearing when they returned; just a handful of ordinary folk heading home with sacks of mandrake and comfrey and jugs of hagathorn scrumpy: village folk who seemed to think nothing of a large black cat dropping out of the sky with a boy upon its back.

And boy he was again, as ordinary as a plain blue day. His nose was its old small self with freckles, his hair once more soft and wavy, his skin as smooth and taut as ever, with a fair fine down.

'Father will be wondering where I am,' Jack said as he dismounted. 'He's bound to be home by now and he told me to stay indoors.'

'He knows where you are,' the cat purred.

'Oh, but I *forgot!*' cried Jack.

'The witches *got* him!
Perhaps they *boiled* him *up!*'

'The witches didn't get him.'

With that, the cat reared up on its hind legs. Its shoulders broadened, its forelegs became strong arms and its whiskers a thick black beard. When its fur turned into clothes, Jack's mouth fell open.

'Father! YOU are the Grand Master?'

'I am,' replied Grimm the woodcutter, 'and have been for many a year, as was my father before me. As you'll be after me, my son.'

'Me?' Jack said. 'Grand Master?'

'You. A Hallowe'en-born child, as was I, and your grandfather.'

'Why didn't you tell me before?'

'You weren't thirteen before. No one under thirteen can enter the charmed circle. And I tell you, if curiosity hadn't sent you after me tonight, you might never have known. Son of mine or not, Hallowe'en's child or no, I would never hand the Grand Mastership on to an incurious heir.'

'Me!' said Jack in wonder. 'Grand Master of all the witches!'

'And warlocks,' his father said. 'But you have much to learn before your time comes. Tomorrow we start your schooling in high magic and tall witchery.'

'Will I also have to be a cat?' Jack asked.

'You can take any form you wish,' said Grimm the woodcutter.

When they reached the ancient oak in which the woodsman's axe was embedded, Grimm snatched the axe and swung it over his shoulder.

'But what about the mistletoe and garlic and the horseshoes you put up every year to keep the witches away?' Jack explained.

'All for the sake of appearances, lad,' his father said.

'That stuff doesn't work.

It never did.

Just another

old witches' tale!'

With this he gave a great guffaw – a laugh such as Jack had never heard from him – and clapped his son on the back. Then home they walked, arm in arm at a lively pace, giving a little skip every now and then, neither of them,

for once,

the least

bit grim!

JACK and the GIANT-KILLER AND JACKWITCH	978 1 40830 774 8
JACK and the BROOMSTICK AND FROM a JACK to a KING	978 1 40830 775 5
JACK-in-the-BOX? AND TALL-TALE JACK	978 1 40830 776 2
JACK FOUR'S JACKDAWS AND JACK of the GORGONS	978 1 40830 777 9

All priced at £4.99